# And Then It Happened

## .. 1 ..

# AND THEN IT HAPPENED

## · 1 ·

M & L Wade

**Books for Boys**

ISBN 0-9731178-0-X


Printed in Canada




Books for Boys
P.O. Box 87
Strathroy ON N7G 3J1

*To All The "Gordons" Out There*

# Contents

# Chapter 1

## The Dead Bird Collection

Our neighbour, Mr. Butterworth, is a kind, elderly man who loves birds. He owns at least fifty birdhouses and just as many birdfeeders and birdbaths. I don't know why we decided to play a joke on Mr. Butterworth, but we did. It was four days into summer vacation and my best friends, Gordon and Paulo, and I were getting a little bored, or maybe we were just restless for some excitement. At any rate, our plan was to collect all the dead birds we could find lying on the side of the road and freeze them. Then, when we had enough dead birds, we

1

would sprinkle them all over Mr. Butterworth's back yard, and he would think his birdseed had poisoned them! This, we thought, would be hilarious.

For days we rode our bikes up and down the local roads searching for unfortunate birds that had been hit by cars. When we got a bag of dead birds, we would ride to Paulo's house and hide the bag in the basement freezer. Our plan almost came to an end when Paulo's mother took out a bag of what she thought was meat and defrosted a big old crow for dinner instead.

When the yelling and shouting were over, we biked our bags of dead birds over to my freezer for safe keeping, and then we planned our attack for the next morning.

First I begged mom to let Paulo and Gordon spend the night.

"I don't know," she said, "Where will you sleep?"

"In the basement," I replied. (*Near the freezer*, I thought). After much begging and pleading, mom caved in.

Next, we set my clock radio for four a.m. We had to get up at the crack of dawn if we wanted to be awake before old Mr. Butterworth, who got up early to watch the birds from his back porch every morning.

The last thing we had to do was defrost the birds.

After making sure my parents had gone to bed, we took our bags of dead birds out of the freezer and set them on top to thaw.

\*       \*       \*

By the cover of dawn the next morning, we tiptoed into Mr. Butterworth's yard and littered his lawn with dead birds. When we were through, it looked like the scene of a horror movie. Dozens of dead birds lay on their backs with their little feet sticking up in the air. Then we crept into the bushes between his property and ours to watch the excitement.

"What time is it?" I asked Paulo.

"Quarter after four," said Paulo, yawning.

We hid in the bushes, not moving and talking little for fear we'd be spotted by the old man's eagle-eyes, or worse, by my parents. Nothing happened for a full fifteen minutes and then I guess we fell asleep, because the next thing I knew, my parents, Mr. Butterworth, several neighbours in pyjamas and four police officers were standing over us, gazing down with a mixture of concern, relief and suspicion.

Apparently, Mr. Butterworth had come out of his house at six a.m. to watch the birds, as usual, but what he saw caused his blood to run cold - dozens of dead birds scattered around his yard and *three dead bodies* half-hidden in the bushes where they had obviously been dragged by some depraved murderer on the loose! Mr. Butterworth had immediately called 911 and the sound of the police sirens had brought my parents and several neighbours over to investigate. Naturally, we boys had some explaining to do.

Our parents and Mr. Butterworth, not to mention the police, did not find our little prank at all amusing. That was the last sleepover Gordon, Paulo and I were allowed to have for a whole month. Our parents also found a solution to our vacation boredom - cutting Mr. Butterworth's lawn (for free!) for the rest of the summer!!

# Chapter 2

## Opening Day

None of us slept well the night before Opening Day. Hey, how could anyone? We had spent weeks sorting through our lures and hooks and bobbers. We'd take them out of our tackle boxes, marvel at them, clean our tackle boxes, and then carefully and strategically reorganize them, item by item. When they were perfect, we would take it all out and start over again. Then there were our rods and reels - we had *real* rods and reels. The days of the kiddie cartoon toy rods were long gone. We inspected them, changed the line, and held practice "casting tournaments" in my backyard to see who was the most accurate and who could cast the furthest. We placed a lawn chair on the deck and pretended it was the front seat of a gleaming bass boat. Of course, on Opening Day, we'd be fishing from the shore. None of us owned a canoe much less a bass boat. After our "casting tournaments," we'd go into the basement and pore over my dad's old fishing magazines or play BassMaster on the computer, all of which only added to our excitement. By Opening Day eve, we just couldn't sleep. It felt like Christmas all over again.

Against her better judgement, my mother had agreed to let Gordon and Paulo, my two best friends and fishing rivals, spend the night at our house. She even consented to letting us sleep outside in the backyard in our family's old canvas tent. Not that we got much sleep. We spent most of the night plotting strategies for catching fish and dreaming of the trophy bass we were no doubt going to land the next day.

6

It was almost dawn when I awoke and saw lights on in the kitchen. *It was time to go!* I nudged Paulo and Gordon, who awoke with a start, and the three of us headed into the house. We wolfed down the pancakes my mother had made us, and then, grabbing tackle boxes, rods and reels, we charged outside to the minivan. We buckled our seat belts and waited. Dad didn't seem to sense our keen anticipation. He wasn't driving with the urgency of a man who knew dawn was breaking, and with it, the "morning feed". We all began to give him subtle driving hints, and we assured him that the police probably weren't even up at this hour, so perhaps he could speed.

Finally we caught a glimpse of the lake, and minutes later, dad pulled off the road into a small gravel parking lot. Seat belts came off, rods and tackle boxes were grabbed. Doors were flung open as the van rolled to a stop and we practically fell over each other in our scramble to get to the water's edge. Each of us wanted to be the first to get a cast in and hopefully catch the first fish. Gordon got the first cast, with Paulo and me right behind him. With rods dangling from our trembling

7

hands, we grinned at each other like it was the last day of school.  We waited for a strike.

Nothing happened.  We changed lures and cast again.  No luck.  We changed lures again.  Still nothing.

"Worms!" Paulo shouted.

"Worms!" Gordon and I yelled back.

Soon, worms were placed on our hooks, sinkers and bobbers attached.  We made our casts and clutched our rods in anticipation of big strikes.  Again nothing happened.  We stared at our bobbers.  They didn't move.  We all reeled in to see if our worms had fallen off.  No, they were still there.  We cast out again for another five minutes of nothing.  We set our rods down on the grass and looked at each other.

"We've been skunked," I said dejectedly.

Gordon brightened then.  "Maybe the fish aren't in the lake," he said.  "Maybe they're all in the creek!"

The creek!  Of course!!  We reeled in and gathered up our gear and raced off toward the creek.

"Creek's low," observed Paulo.  "The only good spot is over there under that tree," he said, pointing to an old, half-dead willow. The bank dropped off sharply under the willow, exposing its roots. The only way to get near the water was to crawl out on a shaky-looking branch high above the creek and cast from there.

"Well, Gordon," I said. "This sure looks like a good spot. Since it was your idea to try the creek, it's only fair that you get to go first."

Gordon, however, did not see it like that. He generously offered, actually *insisted*, that Paulo go first.

"This spot was your idea," Gordon said. "You deserve first chance." Now I've known Gordon since Junior Kindergarten. He wasn't generous then, and he isn't now. Obviously, he was as scared as the rest of us. We argued back and forth over who would get the honour of first cast from the branch. What a bunch of gentlemen we became.

"You first."

"No, *you* first, I insist."

"I double insist!"

"I *triple* insist!!"

Darn! A stalemate. We decided to draw straws

9

(actually pieces of grass) and I lost. I would be the one to test the branch, and *if* it held, to have first cast.

Slowly, I gathered up my rod and approached the tree. Partway up the tree, I heard a snapping sound, and I froze. I gingerly placed a toe on the next branch to test it. Nothing happened. I put my foot on the branch. Still nothing. Encouraged, I hoisted my leg up and put all my weight on it. Hey! It held!! I slowly edged myself out onto the branch 'til I was positioned just right, and I lowered my worm into the water.

*WHAM! A strike!* I set the hook, almost toppling backwards into the water. I lifted the struggling bass out of the water, unhooked it, and tossed it ashore to my buddies, who were yelling "MY TURN! MY TURN!" Generosity had been set aside in favour of bass. I inched my way back while they argued.

"I'm next!"

"I called it first!"

"It was *my* idea."

Apparently Gordon had out-reasoned Paulo by pushing him out of the way and scampering up the tree. He crawled out, lowered his worm, and *SMACK!* A fish! He played it up and tossed it ashore to Paulo, who was drooling with anticipation to get out on the branch. When Gordon climbed down, Paulo jumped on and got into position. He, too, was rewarded with a beautiful large-mouth bass. Then it was my turn again. As I hurried along the branch, I couldn't be sure, but I thought I heard a creaking sound again. I ignored it. The bass were biting! We had three fish on the stringer, soon to be four.

And then it happened. **SNAP!** The branch gave way, and both it and I plunged toward the creek! At the same moment, a fish struck my worm.

I hit the water, sank, surfaced, sank again and resurfaced, still tightly clutching my rod, while Paulo and Gordon hollered instructions from the shore.

"Don't let it get away!"

"Set the hook! *Set the hook!* It's HUGE!!"

I was touched by their obvious concern for my safety. It took me a minute or two to realize that the creek was only a metre deep. I stood up and waded to shore. Unfortunately, in all the excitement, the "big one" had

11

gotten away.

Water sloshed out of my runners with every step as we returned triumphantly to the van, three fish dangling from the stringer.

"You're soaked!" dad exclaimed when he saw me. "Your mother will kill us both if she finds out you fell in."

Next thing I knew, I was wrapped in a car blanket, naked. And there were my shorts, t-shirt and underwear, tied to the van's antenna to dry, flapping in the wind on the drive home.

Opening Day...*there's nothing like it!*

# Chapter 3

## The Hat

One fine summer day, the three of us were hanging out at Paulo's house. Paulo's family owned a small farm, and it was a cool place to be. The farm had cows, a pig, some chickens and a rooster. It was an "Old MacDonald had a farm" kind of place. We were alone in the house. Paulo's father was at work, and his mother had just left for the grocery store. "Be good," she had called over her shoulder as she left.

"Sure. Bye," we mumbled, not even looking up from

our computer game as she pulled the door shut behind her. But the moment the door clicked, we all jumped up and peeked out the window while Paulo's mom backed the car out and disappeared down the long dirt driveway.

"O.K.," said Paulo. "She's gone. Let's snoop!"

Paulo showed us his father's bowling trophies and his power tools in the basement. We held his mom's most expensive china, and basically had a good look at all the stuff in a house that kids are not supposed to touch. While we were snooping through his parents' closet, I noticed a large, round box on the top shelf.

"What's in that box?" I asked, pointing.

"Oh, " exclaimed Paulo, dragging a chair over to the closet. "That's real neat. Let me show you!" He carefully pulled the big box down, placed it on the bed, and removed the lid with an air of satisfaction and importance.

Gordon and I peered into the depths of the box. "But *what is it?*" I asked again.

"It looks like a dead racoon! Cool!" exclaimed Gordon, reaching in for it.

"It is **not**!" shouted Paulo, pushing Gordon aside and reaching in to carefully remove the contents of the box. "It's a hat. Made out of beaver fur." And he held it up for us to see.

"Put it on," I said.

Paulo looked hesitant, as if he shouldn't even be touching it. "I don't know. It cost $800.00. It's my dad's favourite possession," he said.

"Chicken," teased Gordon, grabbing the hat from Paulo and placing it on his own head. We hooted with laughter as Gordon paraded around the bedroom in the hat. It was too big and covered his whole head right down to his nose. I snatched it off his head and did the same, making wild animal sounds, and admiring myself in the mirror.

"Gees, guys! Be careful!" ordered Paulo. "My dad'll kill me if anything happens to his hat."

All of a sudden we heard an ear-splitting sound coming from outside.

"Oh, no! Fire alarm in the barn!!" yelled Paulo. The three of us bolted out of the bedroom and across the back

15

field to the barn. We raced inside and began sniffing the air for smoke and looking for the fire, but found none. Paulo glanced at the alarm, and shook his fist in anger. A barn swallow's nest was perched on top of the alarm, but there was no sign of the bird now.

"Darn birds," he shouted. "They do that every year and give us all heart failure." Quickly he opened a panel on the alarm, punched a few numbers, and the wailing ceased. In the silence we could hear a car coming up the driveway. Paulo's mother was returning from the grocery store, and soon we could hear footsteps coming toward the barn and a voice rang out,

"Was that the alarm I heard coming up the driveway?"

Paulo opened his mouth to answer, when his face suddenly went white. *"Why did you bring that into the barn?!"* He whispered loudly, pointing to my hand. I looked down and was startled to see my hand still firmly gripping Mr. Lima's hat.

"My mom will kill us if she sees that thing down here. Quick! Hide it!!" Paulo ordered. My eyes frantically scanned the barn for a hiding spot.

16

"On that hook," suggested Gordon, pointing to a large nail hammered into a beam about 2 metres off the ground above the pigpen. I quickly jumped on the stall rail and hastily hung up the hat, just as Mrs. Lima's voice grew louder.

"Are you boys in here? You're not up to any trouble, are you? Didn't I hear the alarm?"

We answered "Yes" "No" and "Yes" to her stream of questions. As Paulo explained what had happened with the swallows and the fire alarm, Gordon and I stole quick glances at the hat, resting upon the nail. On and on Paulo talked, when suddenly I noticed the barn door behind his mother gently swinging in the breeze. My eyes widened as the hat also began to swing in the breeze!! Perched up there on the rusty nail, it swayed ever so slightly. Paulo saw it too, and he began talking faster and walking towards the door, hoping to lure his mother out of the barn and away from the hat. And then it happened. Just as they reached the door, a huge gust of wind swept through the barn, and the hat spun around on the nail, hovered in mid air for an agonizing instant, and

17

cannon-balled straight into the pig pen with a resounding *"PLOP!"*

The noise made Paulo's mother turn around and look at Gordon and me suspiciously. We didn't dare move, or even breathe. Big Boy, the occupant of the pig pen, also heard the sound and sloshed over to investigate. *"Maybe it's food"*, he was no doubt thinking. With his huge snout, he sniffed at the hat, driving it deeper into the slop and muck. Then, deciding it was some kind of animal and not dinner after all, he began grunting and whining. Next he let out an ear-splitting squeal and backed away from the hat. He stared at it for a long moment, and then came charging at it full speed.

**"N-O-O-O-O!"** Paulo screamed, running toward the pen and diving in to save the hat.

Gordon and I looked at each other. We were his best friends, and it had been partly our fault (OK, mostly MY fault) that the hat was in the barn in the first place. So in we dove to help save the hat, and to save Paulo from being trampled by an angry pig.

Pigpens are known to be dirty places, and Big Boy's

18

was no exception. Brown ooze covered the floor from one end to the other, but we didn't care. We had to save the hat and our friend. Big Boy lunged at the hat and tore it out of Paulo's wet, slippery hands with his teeth. He then ran victory laps around his pen, kicking up ooze and muck that splattered against us and stuck to our clothes and skin and hair and got in our eyes. With great effort, Gordon managed to fling himself against Big Boy and wrap his filthy arms around the pig's neck. Big Boy was so startled, he tripped head over hocks and took Gordon along for the ride. They somersaulted through the muck, Gordon yelling and Big Boy squealing while Paulo's mother just stared at the spectacle, her mouth open. Another somersault brought Big Boy to his feet again, with Gordon on his back, riding him like a bucking bronco at a rodeo. The pig had never had a rider before, and it was clear he didn't want one now. Faster and faster he tore around his stall, trying to shake Gordon off, while Paulo and I flailed around searching for the hat which was being hopelessly ground into the muck. Finally Big Boy tired of the game, and slowed down enough for Gordon to slide off his back. Suddenly, Paulo spotted the hat in a corner of the stall, and he snatched it up.

"Got it!" he said, spitting something out of his mouth. Then the three of us, dripping muck and pig slop, scampered out of the stall. Big Boy stared at us, grunting and snorting. *We* had the hat, but the pig knew that *he* had won the battle.

Paulo's mom was still frozen to the spot, her hand over her mouth. "W-W-What on earth..?" was all she was able to stammer. Then she noticed the dirty, hairy thing in Paulo's hand. "Please, please, *please* tell me that's not your father's hat!"

Paulo silently handed her the hat, which she carried out of the barn on the end of a broom handle. The three of us looked at each other, too shaken up to speak. And then we burst out laughing, and couldn't stop. Pig slop was in our hair and in our ears. It trickled down our necks and sloshed out of our shoes when we walked. Our jeans were not blue, but brown. We were dirtier and smellier than imaginable. We decided it was safest not to bother Paulo's mom just then, so we hurried outside and jumped into the pond, splashing loudly as we tried to clean ourselves up. While we were bobbing and floating around, Paulo's mother came down to the pond with some old towels, a scrub brush, and soap. Without a word, she left these on the edge of the pond, and went back into the house.

An hour later, and much cleaner, we worked up the courage to go back to the house. What we found relieved and delighted us. There on the kitchen counter was Mr. Lima's prized hat, looking just as new and glossy as when we had pulled it out of the box, and smelling nicely of soap.

"Well," said Paulo's mom. "Now, I can keep a secret as well as anybody. But you know, I think the barn could stand cleaning out, and then the garage needs to be swept, too. And don't forget to feed the chickens, and I'm sure Big Boy is hungry after his ordeal today." She smiled sweetly at the three of us, and we knew we had no other choice. Silently we trooped back out to the barn to begin a long afternoon's work on a fine summer day.

# Chapter 4

## Summer Camp

Parents are funny. Every day of your life since you were little, they've told you: "Watch out for strangers: Don't talk to strangers: Stay away from strangers." Now here we were, the three of us, Gordon, Paulo and I, sitting on a bus, driven by a stranger, being sent to a camp run by (you guessed it) strangers! I said for all we knew, we weren't even going to camp, but were being kidnaped. Paulo said maybe we were being sold into slavery. Gordon said that these strangers were probably taking us to a cow slaughtering house where we would be ground into hamburger, sold to the grocery store, and spend the rest of the summer being barbecued, patty by patty, 'til we'd all been eaten. Gees! Gordon needs help!!

Needless to say, when the bus pulled off the road and drove through a large gateway that said *"Welcome to Camp OutBack"*, we all breathed a sigh of relief. The bus rolled to a stop. We filed off and were greeted by several strangers. The oldest stranger introduced himself as the Head Counsellor, and told us to go straight over to the dining hall for lunch. Another kid rule flashed through my mind: "Never take food from strangers." Five minutes at camp and here we were breaking Kid Rule #2. As luck would have it, lunch was hamburgers. Paulo and I just stared at the meat on our plates. Only Gordon had any kind of appetite.

After lunch, things at camp improved. The Head Counsellor and the rest of the staff told us about the week's events and then we were shown to our rooms. We were to sleep in old wooden cabins, 10 kids to a cabin, 10 cabins in all.

Looking around, Paulo asked "Where's the washroom?"

Our cabin counsellor, Fred, informed us that there was an outhouse down the path from each cabin. *Outhouse?!* Every kid in the room froze and stared at Fred in disbelief. Our parents had sent us to a summer camp with no toilets, only outhouses! What were they thinking?!

The rest of the day was spent getting unpacked and "settling in", as Fred called it. After dinner that evening, we had a large bonfire and the Head Counsellor read us some really hokey, kiddie stories. You know, the kind of stories about baby animals lost in the woods looking for their mothers. In no time, we were yawning, whispering and poking each other, until Gordon interrupted and asked if he could tell a story.

The Head Counsellor smiled and said, "Sure, go right ahead."

I chuckled quietly to myself. The Head Counsellor did not know Gordon like we did.

Clearing his throat, Gordon stood up and said in a loud voice, *"This is the story of the bear and the rabbit."* The

Head Counsellor looked pleased. *"One day,"* continued Gordon, *"a bear and a rabbit were walking in the woods. Suddenly, they both had to go to the bathroom."* The Head Counsellor's smile disappeared. *"After they had both gone to the bathroom, the bear asked the rabbit, 'Do you have a problem with poo sticking to your fur?' 'Not at all,' replied the rabbit. 'Good,' said the bear, and he grabbed the rabbit and wiped his butt with him!"*

Laughter and howling erupted around the campfire. Kids cheered and yelled, "More! More!" The Head Counsellor, however, was furious and sent all us campers to bed early, which was fine by us.

The next few days passed quickly enough. We were kept busy with typical camp activities - swimming, canoeing, crafts, hiking, and playing baseball. Camp life was fun and relaxing, and we were all thoroughly enjoying it. And then it happened.

On the fourth day of camp, a bus pulled up with new campers, and out came the biggest, meanest, scariest-looking kid I ever saw.

"My name's Rex," the giant told us, "and I can beat up

anyone in this crummy camp. Any challengers?"

Not surprisingly, there were none. By the end of the day, Rex had turned our quiet little vacation retreat into a survival course. Rex loved to punch everybody in the arm almost as much as he loved holding kids under water during swimming, or tipping our canoes, or smashing our crafts, but his favourite game was *really* disgusting - booger flicking - and talk about aim! Clearly, something had to be done.

Sitting in our cabin one evening, plotting ways to get back at the bully, I glanced out of the window and noticed Rex lumber out of his cabin and head off down the path toward the outhouse.

"There he goes now," I commented.

All eyes turned and stared at the back of the huge bully as he walked away. Suddenly, an odd look came over Gordon's face, and I knew he was hatching a plot - a devious, demented, deranged, disgusting plot.

In a rush of words, he explained his idea to the rest of us. It was brilliant. Gordon had outdone himself. His idea was pure genius.

None of us slept well that night. The entire cabin was buzzing with nervous whispers about "the plot". The next day, during baseball and swimming, we kept giving each other sly glances and knowing smiles. Word of "the plot" quickly spread through camp, and by dinnertime, it was all set. During the meal, four of the strongest kids in camp snuck out to begin laying the trap. They soon returned and gave Gordon a secret sign that all was in order. I couldn't help glancing at Rex, who was busy stuffing his face with a piece of pie he had stolen from a smaller camper, completely unaware of our plans.

Every night, just after dark, we had a bonfire, sang songs (the Head Counsellor had banned stories) and ate our bedtime snacks. And every night, Rex would steal the snacks from other campers. But tonight would be different.

It was just after dark, and all the campers had assembled around the fire pit. For half an hour we sang songs, while Rex sat and threw stones at the little kids. Finally, the Head Counsellor announced it was snack time, and we all lined up while he doled out cookies and apple juice to everyone. Rex didn't bother getting in line - he never did. He just marched over to the nearest camper with a snack and took it from him. After he gulped down the cookies and juice, he did the same to another nearby camper, and then another. We were used to his routine, and we usually wolfed our food down as quickly as possible to avoid having it stolen. Tonight, however, was different. We all picked at our cookies, and chewed very slowly. We took the tiniest sips of our juice. We made sure there was plenty for Rex to steal. He didn't disappoint us. I kept my eye on him, and counted as he took cookies and juice from 11 campers. That meant he had eaten 33 cookies and drank 11 cups of juice. *Perfect.*

The Head Counsellor picked up his guitar and began playing again. As we sang, we kept glancing at Rex, who was bloated with our bedtime snacks and belching loudly. Halfway through the second song, Rex staggered to his feet and headed off down the path to the nearest outhouse, or at least to what *used to be* the nearest outhouse. And then it happened. The cheery music and tranquility of the night were shattered by the sound of hollering and swearing. *Operation "Move the Outhouse" was a success!!*

Dropping his guitar and turning on his high-powered flashlight, the Head Counsellor raced off down the path, with the rest of us on his heels. Rounding a corner, he suddenly skidded to a stop just inches before a deep, gaping hole in the ground where the outhouse had once stood.

"What the...?" he mumbled. "Where's the outhouse?"

"Right there, sir," said Gordon innocently, pointing a couple of metres further down the path.

**"GET ME OUT OF HERE!"** Rex bellowed from the hole, waist-deep in outhouse output. Soon other counsellors began to arrive on the scene and peered over the edge at Rex, who was covered from head to foot, and vibrating with anger. Finally, someone brought a rope and threw it into the hole. The counsellors grabbed the rope, tug-of-war style, and began to heave, while all the campers watched, thoroughly amused.

"Pull! Pull! Pull!" we all chanted in unison as the

counsellors struggled to lift the hefty bully out of the hole. And then we heard a wet, squelching, sucking sound as Rex was released from the ooze. His face, red with rage, appeared over the top of the hole, and several younger campers quickly scampered off to the safety of their cabins. One last tug and Rex was lifted to safety. His hair was matted down, his clothes dripped brown slime, and he had lost both of his shoes. The stench was overpowering and he seethed with anger. The counsellors immediately marched Rex off to the lake where they forced him, clothes and all, to scrub for an hour.

As the Head Counsellor passed by us on his way back to the bonfire, he flashed us a smile, and that was the last time Rex ever bothered anyone at camp again.

# Chapter 5

## Dead Things

Kids are fascinated by dead things. Adults are afraid of dead things. That's probably because they're so much older and that much closer to death themselves. I don't remember being introduced to dead things. My parents didn't point them out to me the way they pointed out other things when I was little.

"Look, honey, a doggie. Woof, Woof!" they'd say. Hey, I was no dummy. I'd smile and drool and "woof" to anyone when I'd spot a dog. I'd also "moo" and "oink" at

31

the appropriate times, too. Funny thing is, parents never teach us about dead animals. I guess, like Santa Claus, they just hope we don't ask too many questions. Can you imagine your parents slowing down the car and eagerly getting their 2-year-old's attention with "Look, sweetie, a dead racoon!" You'd peer out at the squashed remains, waiting for them to tell you what sound a dead racoon makes, only to find out that a dead animal actually makes no sound at all. With the exception of the occasional dead skunk, dead things are rarely, if ever, pointed out to kids, and the only thing they ever said about dead skunks was "Hold your breath." Apparently, their smell said it all.

Several years ago, when my friends and I were about 8, we came across a skunk in a wood lot near my house. We spotted it and froze, each secretly preparing to run for it and leave the others behind as skunk target. The skunk, however, did not move.

Paulo, the smartest among us, announced, "It's dead." We were fascinated and excited. It was the first dead skunk we'd ever encountered up close. We found a stick and poked our skunk. It was stiff, and we noticed it had no unpleasant odour.

We decided that our skunk deserved a decent burial. We ran to Gordon's house and got his sister's wagon to serve as the funeral car, and then we raced back to the wood lot before some other kids found our skunk and stole it. None of us were brave enough to actually touch the skunk, so we tilted the wagon and pushed it aboard with a stick.

We decided that my backyard would serve as a cemetery. There was a dead patch of lawn in one corner that I knew we could dig up without getting into trouble.

As we walked solemnly home, other kids in the neighbourhood discovered what we were doing and joined us, equally fascinated by the sight of a dead skunk. We finally made it to my backyard. I ran to the shed and got a shovel, and then dug a shallow hole in the earth. We tipped the skunk out of the wagon and into the grave. We all felt quite grown up and responsible. No words were spoken. We simply stared at the skunk in the hole, and I pushed some dirt over it. We all knew we had done the right thing, but now it was over and the funeral broke up, kids dispersing to their own houses. The skunk was soon forgotten. Paulo and Gordon and I played soccer till dinnertime, when we parted company.

At dinner, I answered my parents' usual "What did you do today?" with my usual "Nothing." Then I retired to the family room with my sister to fight over what T.V. show to watch, while  mom did the dishes and dad went outside. A few minutes later I was absorbed in a good show and I didn't hear him start the roto-tiller. Apparently, dad was going to plant some grass seed over the bare patches in the lawn, first churning up the soil with the sharp blades of the roto-tiller. And then it happened. Suddenly we heard a shriek over the sound of the tiller's motor. This was odd. Kids are always shrieking, but dads never shriek. As my sister and I ran into the kitchen to peer out the window, the engine was shut off. What happened next was startling. Dad was staring at the ground. He yelled again and this time I sensed anger. And then, through the open window, it hit us.

"Skunk. Hold your breath!" ordered mom, slamming

the window shut. With a start, I realized what had happened. The blades of the roto-tiller had cut into the skunk's grave and chopped the poor creature up, tearing open what I later learned was a skunk sack and releasing the horrible smell.

I was dead. My father was heading toward the house with a look of extreme anger on his face. He stormed across the yard and stomped up to the back door. I trembled until I heard mom exclaim,

"You're not coming in here smelling like *THAT*!" She led dad to the garden hose and sprayed him with cold water.
"Now scrub!" she ordered, handing him some old rags from the garage. Half an hour later, dad was finally deemed clean enough to come inside and take a bath in tomato juice.

While dad was still in the tub, I quickly explained to mom about our skunk funeral, trying to look as cute and innocent as possible. Mom sighed and took me outside where the two of us quickly buried the remains of the skunk deep in the rose garden, where he would hopefully stay buried for good.

# Chapter 6

## A Bicycle Built for Three

It was the end of September, and we had been back to school for three weeks. Already we were bored and in need of some diversion from homework and tests. When Mr. Evans, the principal, announced that there was going to be a bike race held on the school grounds in two weeks, we were interested. When he mentioned that there would be prizes, we were *very* interested. Signs were posted throughout the school and on poles in the playground. The rules seemed simple enough. Races would be held in heats according to age. There were races for boys, girls, and co-ed (boys and girls together) races. The first one across the finish line in each heat would receive a ribbon and the chance to compete in the final race. There were also going to be lessons in bicycle safety (bor-r-r-ing) and bicycle (yawn) maintenance. Other than that, there were no rules. Any type of bike could enter - mountain bikes, speed bikes, even tricycles. It didn't matter. That's what gave us the idea. Actually it was Gordon's idea. It usually was.

"You know," he said with a look in his eye that meant trouble or excitement (and often both). "the rules don't say anything about the number of riders on each bike."

Puzzled, I pictured Gordon pedalling his mountain bike with Paulo or me perched on the handlebars racing (probably out of control) towards the finish line.

"But that would only slow us down," I said.

"No! Don't you get it?" Gordon practically shouted. "If one kid on a bike can pedal a certain speed, then two kids pedalling the same bike could go twice as fast, and three kids –"

"–*could go three times as fast!*" Paulo finished excitedly.

"But where will we get a bicycle built for three people?" I asked.

"We'll make it!" said Gordon. "Remember when we studied gears and pulleys and all that other stuff? How hard could it be?"

I was doubtful, but Paulo seemed confident that we could actually build such a contraption. His dad was always building strange things in his basement, and it had obviously rubbed off on Paulo.

Early Saturday morning, we met at Paulo's house to begin drawing up plans for our super-bike. We would need three seats, three sets of pedals, three wheels, three chains, and three sets of handlebars. In short, we needed three of everything.

"Where will we get all of this stuff?" I asked.

"No problem," said Gordon cooly. "Our garage is full of bikes. I'll bet my sisters won't even miss them."

I opened my mouth to protest, but Paulo interrupted, "And I have that old bike with the flat tires around here somewhere."

So spare parts weren't a problem.

"Now," said Gordon. "We need a name. How about the *Gordon-mobile*? After all, it *was* my idea."

"How about the *Paulo-mobile*?" returned Paulo.

"How about the -" but I was cut off by Gordon.

"I know!" he shouted. "We'll call it the *Triple Terror*. I heard my dad call the three of us that once."

So now we had a name. All that was left to do was build the bike, I mean the *Triple Terror*. Paulo managed to smuggle some of his dad's tools out of the basement, and I went with Gordon to his house to "borrow" his sisters' bikes.

"Not that pink one, though!" I insisted. "I wouldn't be caught dead riding a pink bike."

We left the pink one behind and headed back to Paulo's house, both of us riding a bike and pushing one between us. By the time we arrived at the Lima farm, we were dead tired, but Paulo was itching to get started.

We disassembled the bikes, including Paulo's old one, and found that we had more than enough parts to get the job done.  I was in charge of the tires, Paulo was in charge of the chains and pedals, and Gordon was just "in charge".  Since it had been his idea, he felt that it was only fair that he got to be the boss.  After a couple of hours of tightening bolts, oiling chains and inflating tires, I was hot, sweaty, greasy, and quite frankly, tired of being bossed around by Gordon.  But it was almost done.  All that was left to do was attach the handle bars and seats, then take the *Triple Terror* on a test run.

Half an hour later, it was finished.  We stood back and proudly surveyed our work.  It was beautiful.  It was awesome.  It was the *Triple Terror*!  Three sets of pedals, three tires, three chains, three seats, three handlebars, and three times the speed.   We were going to be faster than anyone on race day.  No one could beat us!  First-place was ours.  We relished the moment, each of us silent with our dreams.

Gordon spoke first.  "Well, I may as well sit in front, since it was my idea."

"Then I want to be last," said Paulo.  That left me in the middle.

We aimed the *Triple Terror* toward the road and the three of us climbed aboard. Slowly we pumped the pedals until we'd built up a bit of speed, and we steered the bike out of Paulo's driveway and onto the road that led to town.

Faster and faster we pedalled and the *Triple Terror* flew down the road. Gordon's hair whipped back in the breeze, and I could hear Paulo breathing hard behind me. What a sensation; It was unbelievable! Any minute I expected to be launched into outer space!!

Soon we were racing downhill and heading into town. Time to slow down.

As the wind slapped in my face, I yelled "Slow down, Gordon!" Nothing happened. "Slow down," I yelled again. On we whizzed, getting closer to town by the second. "HIT THE BRAKES, GORDON!" I screamed. And then I realized with horror that we hadn't put any brakes on the *Triple Terror*!!

"Back-pedal! Back-pedal!" I shouted. Our feet frantically flew around backwards, but nothing happened. There was no resistance, no slowing down. Stealing a glance around Gordon, I could see an intersection ahead, *and the light was red!* I broke out into a cold sweat and closed my eyes. When I opened them, the light was green. Beautiful green! We whizzed through the intersection, people's heads turning to stare as our strange contraption flew by. Somewhere behind us, a siren began to wail. It was the police! *Now we were in trouble.* Wasn't there some law about having to pull over when the police were chasing you? But we couldn't stop even if we'd wanted to. Cars swerved and people jumped out of our way as the *Triple Terror* raced through town, and then with horror, I realized that we were headed straight toward the river at the end of the road.

*BUMP!* The *Triple Terror* left the pavement and sailed across the grass. Another bump and we were on the dock heading right for the water. Time slowed down, and everything seemed to happen in slow motion. Two old men sat on lawn chairs at the end of the dock, fishing rods dangling limply from their hands.

"**LOOK OUT!**" we all shouted.

The startled men turned around, instant fear filling

their faces. And then it happened. I closed my eyes as the *Triple Terror* came to the end of the dock and sailed through the air, plunging us into the cold, deep water. Gordon, Paulo and I came up sputtering and coughing. The head of one old fishermen popped up beside me, and then the other. The five of us bobbed around in the water, momentarily stunned. The police cruiser skidded to a stop on the gravel near the boat-launch beside the dock, its siren still wailing. We swam toward the boat launch and crawled out of the water. The *Triple Terror* was gone, sunk -- just like the Titanic on her maiden voyage!

After we apologized to the fishermen, the police insisted on taking us home. We shivered together in the back of the police cruiser, lucky to be alive.

"Do you know how fast you kids were going?" demanded the officer. "I clocked you on my radar doing 60 in a 40 zone!"

Sixty kilometres an hour! Cool! We'd have won that race for sure!

I wondered if there were enough spare parts left to build the *Triple Terror Two*?

# Chapter 7

## The Great Egg Fight

Gordon, Paulo and I were sitting in our clubhouse in my backyard trying to come up with ways to raise money - lots of money. We had accidentally destroyed Gordon's sisters' bikes last weekend trying to make a really fast bike that would win all the prizes at the school bike rally. Now, the *Triple Terror*, as we had called our bicycle built for three, was lying at the bottom of the river, rusting away, and Gordon's parents insisted that we replace the girls' bikes with our own money. My parents and Paulo's had agreed, and so here we were, sitting in my backyard, depressed and nearly broke.

"How much money did you say you had in your sock drawer?" Gordon asked me for the third time.

"Same as the last time you asked," I replied wearily. "Five dollars and forty-five cents."

"And I have eight dollars," replied Gordon. "What about you, Paulo. You're the rich one, selling all those eggs."

Paulo had an egg stand at the end of his driveway, and he was allowed to gather up all the eggs that his family didn't need and sell them to people driving by his family's farm.

"But I only sell about three dozen a week. I'm not that rich. Right now I have sixteen dollars saved, and it's taken me over a month to get that much. We'll never be able to sell enough eggs to buy three new bikes!"

"Who likes eggs, anyway," grumbled Gordon. "The only thing eggs are good for is..." he stopped and sat up straight. "I've got it!" he cried. "I know how we're going to get rich in a hurry!"

Gordon explained his plan to us, and we all agreed that it was a sure-fire way to earn back the money for the bikes.

The following Monday, Paulo got off the school bus carrying a dozen eggs carefully wrapped in a towel to make sure they wouldn't break. We quickly set to work, scattering eggs all over the schoolyard where we knew kids would find them. We knew that kids would only do one thing with eggs - throw them at each other!

After setting the trap, we stood back at the edge of the yard and waited. First one kid, then another found an egg, and within a few minutes, every kid was running around trying to find eggs faster than an Easter egg hunt. And then it happened. Someone threw the first egg, and it smacked right into another kid, covering his back with runny yolk and broken shell. The kid turned around to see who had hit him, but couldn't tell who had done it, so he just whipped his egg at the kid standing closest to him, and that set off a chain reaction. Our egg fight was born! Kids ran about searching for more eggs while others wiped egg from their clothes, hair and back-packs. What

47

a mess we had started!  Soon, all twelve eggs had been found and thrown, but kids were still frantically looking for more, and everyone was excited.

During the next recess, the egg hunt continued, but of course, no more eggs were found.

"If I had an egg," I heard an older kid exclaim, "I would crack it on the head of the jerk who hit me this morning."

I seized the opportunity and ran up to him.  "I know where you can get a whole dozen eggs!"

He eyed me suspiciously for a moment.  "Where?"

"From my friend tomorrow morning.  He lives on a farm and raises chickens.  But it'll cost you."

"How much?" he asked eagerly.

"Just one dollar for each egg."

"Sold!" the kid cried.

And that is how we managed to sell dozens of eggs. The next day, Paulo's dad drove him to my house.  Paulo got out of the van carrying a large box containing 100 eggs, every egg that he could gather on his farm, including the ones his family normally kept for themselves.  Gordon arrived to help us carry the eggs to school.

"What'd you have for breakfast this morning?" I asked Paulo.

"Not eggs!" he replied.  "We ate cereal instead."

"And your mom actually thinks that kids are buying eggs to *eat*?" asked Gordon

About a block from the school, we stopped and waited. There we met all the kids who had agreed to buy our eggs, and before we knew it, we had $100.00 in our hands. This was amazing!  At this rate, we would have the money for the bikes by the end of the week!  We tucked the money away deep in our pockets and ran to school to take tomorrow's egg orders.

When we got there, we were shocked at what we saw. We hadn't thought about the mess that nearly a hundred eggs would make.  There was egg yolk running down trees and poles, smashed shells on the swings and slide. Eggs dripped down windows and doors.  The bricks were smeared with runny, messy eggs, and kids dripped with egg.  The entire playground looked like a giant , runny omelette. The principal was walking around the school yard, surveying the damage. He did not look happy. And then it happened. Someone threw an egg, and it hit the principal right on the back of his big, bald head. Perfect aim, I had to admit, but I knew we were in big trouble as egg dripped off the man's head and ran down his collar. His face was red with rage, and he ordered everyone to get in line immediately.

"Where did you get these eggs?" demanded the principal when everyone was in line.

All eyes turned to face Gordon, Paulo and me, standing perfectly still at the back of the line.

"From them," said a voice, and 300 fingers all pointed at us.

Wiping egg off his face, the principal grabbed us by our jackets and marched us into his office while the entire school stared after us. Half an hour later, we sat in the office with our parents, who had arrived to take us home for our three-day suspension.

Everyone was furious, so furious, in fact, that they never thought to ask if we actually *sold* the eggs or just *gave them away* for kids to throw. Of course, Gordon, Paulo and I were not going to say anything about selling the eggs unless we were asked. We just looked at each other silently and grinned behind our parents' backs as we were led out of the school.

# Chapter 8

## Turkey in the Straw

It was one week before Thanksgiving, a time we had all been dreading. We were dreading Thanksgiving because that meant that Paulo's dad would soon be cutting off Spot's head. You see, Spot was a turkey. Paulo's dad bought him in the spring when he was a tiny, fluffy poult with the plan to raise him on the farm and then eat him for Thanksgiving dinner. At first, this seemed like a fine idea, but that was before we really got to know Spot. This was not your typical turkey. He acted more like a dog

52

than a turkey. One day while Gordon and I were playing catch with Paulo in the field near the barn, we discovered that the turkey could fetch...and he was good at it. He'd chase after the ball when one of us would miss it, and using his wings and his beak, he would roll the ball back to us and deposit it at our feet. It was then that Paulo came up with the idea of naming him Spot. Paulo had always wanted a dog, but his mother was allergic to them, so Paulo thought it would be fun to train the turkey like a dog instead. We taught Spot to shake a claw and to sit. He would come when we whistled, and everyday when Paulo got off the school bus, there was Spot, waiting at the end of the driveway for him. Paulo's dad warned us not to get too attached to "the bird". (He refused to call him "Spot").

"This is a farm, and that bird is our Thanksgiving meal," he told us repeatedly. Deep down we all knew this, but we grew quite fond of Spot in spite of it, or maybe because of it. The thought of Spot lying helpless in a roasting pan stuffed with sage and onion was too much to bear, but what could we do? We tried whining, begging and pleading, and we even offered to buy Paulo's family a store-bought turkey for Thanksgiving, but Paulo's dad stood his ground. Spot was a goner.

Three days before Thanksgiving, Paulo got off of the bus and was greeted by Spot as usual, but he was surprised to see a police car in the driveway. Was something wrong? Paulo ran to the house and overheard a tall, skinny policeman saying "...Looks like they entered the barn through an unlocked door. Did a lot of damage, and stole about 40 chickens. Lucky they didn't set fire to the place. This is the third break-in this month in the area".

After the policeman left, Paulo's dad explained that there was someone, maybe a small gang, going around breaking into barns, scaring the livestock, stealing chickens and making a real mess. The police were warning farmers to keep their barn doors locked, and to keep a close eye on them at night.

"If only we had a watch-dog," Paulo's dad murmured to himself. And that gave Paulo an idea. When he phoned Gordon and me, we jumped on our bikes and pedalled over to the Lima farm as fast as we could, ready to help. We had just three days left to train Spot to become the world's best watch-turkey.

Paulo decided that the most important thing to teach Spot was to sit in front of the barn at night, just like a watch-dog, and to gobble really loudly if anyone came near. Scooping up Spot, we carried him to the front of the barn, and sat him down on the ground.

"Stay!" commanded Paulo, and walked away. Spot followed him. Paulo carried Spot back to the front of the barn and sat him down again with a firm "stay", and he walked away. Again Spot followed him.

"Show him what you mean," I said. "Let's sit Gordon down in front of the barn and tell him to stay. Then Spot'll see what you want him to do." So Paulo and I carried Gordon to the front of the barn, and sat him down firmly on the ground.

"Stay!" commanded Paulo, and Gordon obeyed. Then it was Spot's turn again, and again he followed when Paulo walked away. Three more unsuccessful attempts were made before Paulo gave up.

"You dumb old bird," grumbled Paulo. "Don't you wanna be saved?" We all looked sadly at Spot, and then we put him in the barn and headed back to the house.

The next day after school, we tried to teach Spot how to attack. Gordon and I practised our best boxing moves, hoping Spot would get the idea, but he just didn't catch on. We tried wrestling, but that didn't work, either. In a flash of inspiration, I head-butted Gordon in the stomach, pretending my nose was a beak. Gordon yelled and fell backwards, and pain seared through my nose. Still Spot didn't catch on. Dejectedly, we went back into Paulo's house. We were running out of time.

The night before Thanksgiving, we all trudged down to the barn to sit with Spot and to try to come up with a new way to train him. We had run out of ideas and were feeling very depressed about the whole thing.

"You were a good pal, Spot," I said. "I'm really gonna miss you."

"It was nice knowing you, Spot," said Gordon.

Paulo was really having a hard time saying good-bye to Spot. Gordon and I quietly left the barn so the two of them could be alone for a few minutes, knowing that the next time we saw Spot, it would be between two slices of bread in Paulo's sandwich at school.

A few minutes later, Paulo joined Gordon and me on the porch.

"Since tomorrow's a school holiday," he said, "do you think your folks would let you sleep over?" Clearly, Paulo needed cheering up.

"Sure," we agreed, and after a few phone calls, the arrangements were made.

Mrs. Lima made popcorn and we watched a movie, but Paulo hardly laughed, even at the good parts. We played computer games for about an hour, and then it was time for bed. Gordon and I told Paulo all of our best jokes, but Paulo still didn't crack a smile. It was no use, so we just turned out the light and fell asleep. And then it happened.

Just after midnight, we awoke to a shrill screeching sound from somewhere outside, followed by a yelping noise that sounded almost human. Paulo's parents must have heard it, too, because we almost collided with Mr. Lima in the hallway as we raced downstairs to investigate.

Mr. Lima was wearing his boxer shorts and an undershirt, and he carried a baseball bat.

"What's that noise?" he demanded, and then we heard it again.

"It's Spot!" cried Paulo. Somebody's hurting Spot!"

We ran down to the barn, in our pyjamas and bare feet. As we got closer, the yelping grew louder.

"Don't hurt me! Get away! Shoo!" a frightened voice was pleading.

Mr. Lima threw open the barn door and hit a switch. Suddenly the barn was flooded in light. The four of us stood there, gaping in surprise at the scene before us. A man with a mask over his face was crouched in a corner of the barn, cowering behind a bale of straw. Spot was flapping his wings and pecking at the man, keeping him pinned down, all the while gobbling and shrieking at the top of his lungs. *Spot had captured the chicken bandit, and he had saved the farm from being robbed!!* That made him a hero. Even the police officer who arrived at the barn when Paulo called 911 agreed that Spot had managed to do what four police officers had failed to do.

A reporter from the local newspaper even took Spot's picture. In the background, you could see Mr. Lima looking as proud as if he had trained Spot himself.

That clinched it. Mr. Lima said that Spot could stay and be the new watch-turkey. After all, how could anyone eat a hero?

As for Thanksgiving dinner, Paulo's family ordered Chinese food instead.

# Chapter 9

## Halloween

*"The halls of the old school were pitch black. Children groped their way along the corridors, many for the last time. Licking my parched, cracked lips, I extended a trembling hand toward the water fountain. I turned the knob and instantly recoiled as a geyser of warm blood spewed forth, splattering my face and soaking my T-shirt. Upon entering the classroom, I was stunned to notice not chalk at the blackboard, but bony, white severed fingers. I felt a scream of panic rising in*

*my throat, and then it happened..."*

"That will be all, Gordon!" interrupted Mrs. Hoagsbrith.

"But I'm not finished," said Gordon, standing at the front of the classroom, a rumpled piece of paper in his hands.

"Take your seat," the teacher insisted firmly. "Sarah, will you please stand and share your Halloween story with the class?"

For the next half hour, we were bored by silly stories of dancing pumpkins, laughing skeletons and black cats, but I wasn't listening. I was daydreaming about Halloween. Tonight was the big night, the night we'd waited for our whole lives. For the very first time, Gordon, Paulo and I were allowed to go trick-or-treating by ourselves - no parents, and no little sisters tagging along! Just the three of us on a mad, wild dash to collect as much candy as humanly possible in one evening. For weeks, we'd plotted our strategy, debated over pillow-cases versus heavy-duty garbage bags, tested our flashlights and planned our route. It was going to be perfect. The recess bell startled me out of my daydream, and fifteen minutes later, we were back in our seats, sweaty from a vigorous game of soccer.

"Now class," said Mrs. Hoagsbrith when we had quieted down. "It's time for our annual pumpkin-carving contest, thanks to Paulo's father who grew all these pumpkins on his farm especially for us." She beamed at Paulo.

Each student was given a pumpkin and for the next hour we were kept busy scooping out seeds, carving faces and turning our pumpkins into Jack-o-lanterns. Mrs. Hoagsbrith circled the room, admiring our efforts and making encouraging sounds, until she came to Gordon's pumpkin, a large pumpkin with a single hole carved near the bottom.

Drawing a deep breath, she asked "Gordon, is this all you've done? Why, it doesn't even have eyes! What kind of a Jack-o-lantern is this?"

She leaned closer to examine it. The class quickly gathered around Gordon's desk.

Proudly, Gordon announced, "It's a vomiting

pumpkin!" And with that, he pushed the top of the pumpkin firmly down, causing a stream of pumpkin seeds and pulp to spray out of the hole of the overstuffed Jack-o-lantern and send a runny mess of "pumpkin vomit" spewing in all directions. Some kids shrieked, but others looked at Gordon in admiration. *Why didn't I think of such a cool idea?* they were no doubt wondering. Our teacher just sighed and pointed toward the door.

By the time Gordon returned with a mop and bucket, it was almost time to go home.

"You won, Gordon!" somebody announced. "We voted, and everyone agreed your pumpkin was the best." Mrs. Hoagsbrith didn't say a word as she handed Gordon a big red ribbon and a large pack of Chewy-Chewy bubble gum.

"Meet me at my place at four to help me finish my chores!" Paulo called to Gordon and me as he boarded his bus.

At home, I quickly gathered up my pillow-case, costume, and flashlight, and at 3:59 exactly, we pulled up in front of Paulo's house. My dad was still giving me a list of last-minute instructions as long as my arm as I got out of the car.

"Don't eat anything before we check it. Don't stay out past 8:30. You three stick together, and keep your flashlights on. And stay away from strangers."

"Sure, dad! Bye!" *Gees, did he think I was a baby?* I slammed the car door and ran up the front steps to Paulo's house.

Gordon was already there, and the two of us quickly helped Paulo finish his chores. When the chickens had finally all been fed, we raced back to the house to get into our costumes. Paulo's mom always made him the best costumes. This year he was dressed as a pirate, with an earring and a patch over one eye and a really neat hook. He even had a fake wooden leg that his dad had made in his shop in the basement. When people saw Paulo standing at their door on Halloween, they always "oohed" and "aahed" over his costume, and he usually got extra candy. I, on the other hand, was wearing what I have worn since I was six. I was a hockey player. With my mom's old eyebrow pencil, I made a big bruise under one eye, and I carried a hockey stick. I wore my Maple Leafs sweater with the big blue leaf on the front and number 13 on the back. Mats Sundin was my favourite player. *I* never got extra candy, unless someone was a Leafs fan, too. Gordon's costume was always a mystery until the last minute. He tried to outdo himself every year, and he never failed to come up with something really morbid. Sometimes I think he even scares the parents who are handing out the candy. Tonight, Gordon was wearing his grandmother's old, matted fake-fur coat. It hung to his ankles, and was splattered with red paint. Running down the back of the coat were two greasy black tire tracks. On his face he smeared dirt and more black grease. Paulo and I stared at the odd get-up as Gordon spun around in front of us, showing off his costume.

"Get it? I'm road-kill!" he announced proudly. We admired his costume. Only gory Gordon could have come up with such a gruesome idea.

After a hurried dinner, we left Paulo's house and ran across the front lawn.

"Hey, guys," Paulo said when we reached the road.

"It'll be faster if we cut across Mr. McGregor's field. That way, we'll get to the houses sooner and collect more loot!" I looked at Gordon. Mr. McGregor's field was full of tall, dried-out cornstalks taller than us. I wasn't sure we could find our way in the dim twilight, but Gordon said "Sure", and we crossed the road, Paulo's wooden leg clacking on the pavement.

The moon was just rising - a thin yellow crescent that gave off little light. Switching on our flashlights, we pushed our way noisily through row after row of dried corn. Paulo was in the lead, and we followed him faithfully for about ten minutes before any of us spoke.

"Say, Paulo," I inquired nervously. "You sure you know where we're going?"

"Of course he does," replied Gordon. "He's a farm kid, isn't he?"

Paulo didn't say anything. He just kept pushing his way through the cornstalks. Another five minutes passed, and Paulo slowed down.

"Uh, guys," he said quietly. "Would either of you like to lead? I think we're almost there."

"Just what I thought!" I shouted. "We're lost!"

"How could you have gotten us lost?" demanded Gordon. "You said you knew the way!"

"I do," said Paulo. "In the daytime. Now that it's dark..." His voice trailed away.

"Great," I sighed. "Just great." A large black cloud skidded in front of the moon, and the wind began to ripple through the cornstalks. "What do we do now?"

"Well," said Paulo, pointing to the left. "We came from that way. So let's try this way." He shone the beam of his flashlight to the right. Gordon and I didn't move. "Come on, guys," pleaded Paulo. "It has to be the way."

Since there was no other way to go, we headed to the right.

In a short time, Gordon gasped and yelled "Footprints! Look. Footprints. Someone's out here!" I bent over to examine the ground, and sure enough, there were several sets of footprints in the soft earth. And then I noticed small holes in the dirt at even intervals between some of the footprints. I glanced at Paulo's wooden leg.

"You dummy! These are our footprints. We're going

67

in circles."

By now it was getting windier and I began to shiver in my hockey sweater. "Halloween's probably half over," I said sadly. "By the time we get out of here, it'll be too late to get much candy."

Paulo said he thought we'd be stuck here all night, wandering around in circles. "They'll find our stiff, cold bodies in the morning and have to rush us to the hospital!"

But Gordon said he doubted if anyone would ever be able to find us, we were so deep in the cornfield. "Mr. McGregor will harvest his field with his giant, man-eating tractor and we'll be shredded into corn flakes, shipped off to a cereal processing plant, lightly-toasted, vacuum-sealed in a box, and enjoyed by hungry kids every morning till we've been completely devoured!"

"Shut up, Gordon," said Paulo nervously.

"Yeah, quit scaring us!" I added.

Suddenly, the night was filled with a blood-curdling shriek that caused us all to jump.

"W-What was that?" stammered Paulo, moving closer to Gordon and me. The horrible shriek rang out again,

68

and the three of us started to run. Faster and faster we ran through the field, stalks of corn catching at our clothes and slapping in our faces. Thunder rumbled low in the distance. My legs grew heavy and my breathing came hard. My heart pounded in my chest. I stumbled, got up and ran on. Paulo was right behind me, and Gordon, tripping and stumbling along in the big fur coat, was several paces behind us. Before long we came to a small clearing in the field and stopped, panting, trying to catch our breath.

"That was c-close," said Gordon when he caught up with us. More thunder, this time closer, rumbled threateningly, and then there came a soft scratching sound, barely audible. Gordon heard it first. Then Paulo and I heard it, too. We stared at each other, rooted to the spot with fear. The scratching got louder, as whatever was out there with us came closer. We stood huddled together, shivering, hardly daring to breath. Lightning forked across the sky, and the cornstalks rustled. Again, the crazed shriek rang out, closer than before. The skin on the back of my neck prickled, and cold sweat trickled down my back. And then it happened. The cornstalks in front of us parted. A flash of lightning streaked across the sky, illuminating the clearing. In the light I could see a huge creature emerging from the rows of corn. Giant wings fanned out, and with another terrifying shriek, the creature lunged at us. Paulo and I jumped out of the way, and the creature hurled itself at Gordon, with claws extended and wings furiously flapping. Gordon fell backwards and struggled to get up in the long fur coat. He screamed and tried to kick. The creature hissed and pecked at him with its beak and began to gobble Gordon up! *Gobble him up?*

"Wait a minute!" shouted Paulo. "It's Spot!!" Upon hearing his name, the overstuffed pet turkey turned toward Paulo.

"Get it off me! Get it off me!" Gordon yelled, still writhing on the ground. Paulo whistled and Spot jumped off Gordon and waddled over to his owner.

"What are you doing here?" Paulo asked the pet turkey as I helped Gordon to his feet. The fur coat had protected him from the worst of the turkey's attack.

Paulo laughed. "Spot must've thought you were a wild animal chasing me. He wanted to protect me. Good turkey."

"Some watch-dog," said Gordon sulkily, brushing dirt and pieces of cornstalk off his costume. Spot began to waddle off through the field, and then he stopped and let out another piercing yell.

"Come on," said Paulo. "I'll bet he knows the way out! He wants us to follow him."

Sure enough, Spot led the three of us out of the field, and in less than five minutes, we emerged on the road across from Paulo's house.

"Oh, no," said Gordon. "That dumb old bird led us right back where we started."

At that moment, Paulo's mother stuck her head out the front door. "I thought that was you boys," she yelled across the road. "And right on time. It's 8:30. How responsible you are."

*Responsible? Right on time?* We stared at each other in disbelief. We had spent the entire night stuck in a cornfield, and never even trick-or-treated a single house!

71

How would we ever live this down?

We looked at our empty, limp pillow-cases and vowed never to take a shortcut again.

# Chapter 10

## The Christmas Disaster

It was everyone's favourite time of year, Christmas - a time when it is better to give than to receive, or so the saying goes. Don't you believe that! My friends and I don't, and we don't think anyone else does, either. Let's face it: Kids don't have much money, so we *can't* give, but we sure can receive! I could easily receive every toy and game in an entire shopping mall. Every kid I know is a natural receiver. I've never met a kid who is a natural *giver*. Kids aren't even good sharers, but that's another story. That's why when our teacher, Mrs. Hoagsbrith, gave the class an assignment to write down what we wanted for Christmas and why we wanted it, I knew it would mean extra homework, and every other kid in the class knew it, too. We let out a loud, collective groan, which our teacher pretended not to hear. Instead, she smiled and said she had some good news for us. This year, she told us, our class had been chosen to put on the annual school Christmas play. This, too, was met by groans from some of the students. Ignoring them, Mrs. Hoagsbrith began handing out copies of the script, explaining that we would read it together as a class.

"This way," she said, "I can decide who will play each part." She started calling on kids to read. When she got to me, I mumbled my lines and made mistakes on purpose. There was no way I was going to be chosen to play a part. I didn't want to waste valuable recess time memorizing lines and practising Christmas carols. Paulo, the best reader in the class, must have guessed what I was doing, because he, too, stumbled over words and lost his place twice. Mrs. Hoagsbrith sighed and wrote something down on her clipboard. Paulo turned around and grinned at me. We were safe. Several more students read, and then it was Gordon's turn. What happened next took the whole class by surprise, including Mrs. Hoagsbrith. Gordon read the lines so well and with such enthusiasm that the class actually applauded. Mrs. Hoagsbrith, looking quite shocked, said, "I may regret this, but Gordon, you'll be Santa Claus in our play." Then she added, "And to see that everything goes smoothly, I'll be Mrs. Claus." Then she sighed again and that's how it all began.

Paulo was chosen to play Rudolph, a non-speaking part. He just had to nod his head and press a little battery-operated switch in his pocket to make his nose light up. Just when I thought I was completely off the hook, Mrs. Hoagsbrith announced that those of us not chosen to be in the play would all have equally important jobs. We were to design and paint the sets. Another groan rumbled through the classroom. There goes recess.

For the next few weeks, we were kept busy learning lines, practising Christmas carols and painting sets.

Parents sewed costumes, and everything progressed according to schedule. Then, one day, Mrs. Hoagsbrith rushed into the gym at recess with a huge smile on her face. The local cable channel, she announced breathlessly, was going to come to our school and film our play. We were going to be on T.V.!

Everyone began talking at once, and Gordon, who had the lead, shouted,

"HO! HO! Hollywood, here I come!"

We all worked feverishly from that moment on. Our play had to be perfect! For days, I painted snowmen and elves, Christmas trees and Santa's workshop, and then all too soon, the big night arrived.

Behind the scenes, there was great commotion. The library had been turned into a dressing room. Teachers shouted orders, and mothers put make-up on the actors, even the boys. The stage crew tended to dozens of last minute details.

"Fix the star!" barked Mr. Werner, the stage manager. "It's crooked."

"Where are the stockings? We have to have

stockings!" shouted Mrs. Hoagsbrith.

Gordon, who had escaped the embarrassment of having to wear make-up because of his beard and mustache, was dressed and in the gym early.

"Here", I yelled, tossing him a tube of super-glue. "Help me hang these stockings by the chimney."

"With glee," he replied. *Oh, brother! Gordon was taking this acting thing way too seriously.*

Suddenly it was 6:30 and families began to arrive. At 6:40, the camera crew from the local T.V. station arrived. At ten minutes to seven, the school band started playing Christmas carols.

"Two minutes 'til curtain. Hurry, everyone!" Mr. Werner called in a loud whisper. I leapt off the stage as the elves came and took their places. Gordon quickly slapped the last stocking into place, slipped the tube of super-glue into his pocket, and got into position. The curtain rose, the T.V. cameras rolled, and the elves began to sing.

I had to admit that Gordon did a wonderful job as Santa, even if he and Mrs. Hoagsbrith did make a lopsided pair as Mr. And Mrs. Claus.  Clearly, our teacher had worried for nothing, *or had she?*

While Gordon was busy smiling and hamming it up and HO-HO-HOing for the camera, the tube of super-glue in his pocket sprung a small leak, and a little bit of glue oozed out through the end of the tube - so little that no one, including Gordon, noticed it, even when some of the sticky stuff got on his glove.

The play was drawing to an end.  All Gordon had to do was pat Rudolph on the head, climb aboard his sleigh, and take off.  It all sounded so simple.  Too simple, in fact, for when Gordon patted poor Paulo on the head, his glove stuck to Paulo's costume and he couldn't let go.  He tugged his hand.  *Blink, blink, blink* went Rudolph's red nose.  Gordon pulled harder.  *BLINK, BLINK* went Rudolph.

Everyone was watching Santa, and people in the audience started to whisper and giggle.  Mrs. Hoagsbrith shot Gordon a look that said, *"What are you doing??"* Gordon tugged one last time, but he was clearly stuck to Rudolph.

"Well, Rudolph," said Gordon thinking quickly. "I've grown very attached to you lately. How about riding with me in my sleigh instead of pulling it?"

*Blink, blink, blink* went the nose. The two of them headed toward the sleigh, but stopped short. The sleigh only had one seat in it! It was meant for Santa, not Santa and Rudolph! In a flash of brilliance, Gordon said, "HO-HO-HO! Rudolph, wouldn't you like to sit on my lap and tell me what you want for Christmas? Have you been naughty or nice, Rudolph?"

*Blink, blink, blink, blink!!*

So into the sleigh climbed Santa and Rudolph, the reindeer sitting on Santa's lap. Paulo's weight caused more super-glue to squirt out of Gordon's pocket. The audience was laughing out loud now as Mrs. Hoagsbrith came out to deliver the final lines of the play. She opened her mouth to speak, and then it happened. There was a loud SNAP followed by a splintering sound. Santa's sleigh was breaking under the weight of the two boys, and suddenly Rudolph and Santa flew out of the sleigh and hurled toward Mrs. Claus. In the commotion, more glue spewed from Gordon's pocket, landing on several of the dancing elves. There was a ripping sound, and Paulo's costume was torn from his body as he and Gordon were hurled in opposite directions. Paulo's reindeer costume dangled from Gordon's glove as he flew helplessly toward Mrs. Claus and head-butted her from behind. Maybe I should have said face-butted because when the dust settled, there was Gordon, his left cheek firmly glued to our teacher's rear-end. Elves were stuck together, too, and poor Paulo stood on stage wearing nothing but his underwear, a pair of antlers and a blinking nose.

The audience roared with laughter, and I think I saw one of the camera-men wipe a tear from his eye. Every kid on stage, every reindeer and elf, and the entire school choir stood staring at the spectacle with their mouths and eyes gaping. They were too mortified to even laugh. Their perfect play had been ruined and the T.V. camera was capturing every detail on film!

Mrs. Hoagsbrith sighed and shouted above the noise in the gym. "Merry Christmas to all!"

And from behind her came Gordon's muffled voice.

"And to all a good night!"

    The curtain dropped.

# About the Authors

**Michael Wade** was born a long time ago, in a place far, far away. He grew up in London, Ontario and currently lives in Strathroy, Ontario. Michael enjoys hunting, wilderness canoeing and working out.

**Laura Wade** was born not quite so long ago and not as far away as Michael. She, too, was raised in London, Ontario and currently resides in Strathroy, where she works as a Children's Librarian.

*Catch All The Exciting Adventures*
*of Gordon, Paulo and Me!*

Order the complete
***And Then It Happened***
series today.

For details on ordering books,
student activities, new stories and more,
visit us at our Web Site
# www.boysbookshelf.com